Maggie and the Selkie

Heather Ewings

Quamby Press

Chapter 1

That morning the bodies were counted. Twelve in all, and one still missing.

Hamish.

When the families took the bodies home to prepare them for burial, Maggie sneaked down to the beach to walk the shoreline. Five miles north, and five miles south. Through her tears, every piece of driftwood and kelp was a human figure; an arm reaching for help, a crumpled body found too late. Maggie's hope disappeared with the sun and a low, slow groaning emerged from her throat as she sank to the sand. The pain in her heart was so strong she didn't notice the water rising around her, the cold seeping into her skin.

She thought of her dream of the previous night, of thrashing seas and the stabbing hollow in her chest.

'I saw what was to come. I should've made him stay!' She squeezed her eyes shut, tears slipping over her cheeks to add to the salty water about her knees.

'And how would you have made a fisherman stay when there was food to be caught for his village?'

Maggie started, tripping backwards in her haste to get up and landing awkwardly on a wrist as the waves splashed around her.

The man before her stood knee deep in water, his bare legs protruding from a strange coat that hung around his shoulders.

'Perhaps I can help you?' He held out a hand, and Maggie took it, the warmth of his grip waking her up to the fact that her body was numb.

He pulled her towards him and carried her the few steps out of the water to above the high-tide mark. He sat her down at a pile of sticks, and she was aware of him doing *something* before her. When a flash sparked a fire, and she realised what he'd been up to.

'We need to get you out of these wet clothes.'

Maggie should have felt embarrassed at a strange man undressing her, but there was nothing as he peeled off her dress and undergarments, wrapping her in his cloak before spreading her clothes out across sticks wedged in the sand.

He disappeared for a time. Maggie must have dozed, for when she woke the fire was loaded up with logs, crackling and popping from the heat. She sat up, and held her hands out to the warmth.

'You feel better?' His voice was deep, and when Maggie looked up she realised he wasn't wearing a stitch of clothing. Her cheeks burned as she averted her eyes.

'You need your coat.' She went to remove it from her shoulders, but he held out a hand and stopped her.

'Not as much as you do.'

'Aren't you cold?' she asked, staring into the flames to avoid looking at him.

'No.'

'How did you find me? Where did you come from?'

'You called me,' he said.

'I called you?' Maggie frowned. 'How?'

'You cried seven tears into the sea.'

Vague memories surfaced of tales her grandmother had shared with her as a child. She stood up, and met his gaze. 'You're a selkie?'

He nodded. 'I am.'

'You live under the waves, out there.' She gestured to the sea.

'I do.'

Hope quickened her pulse. 'Can you bring someone back?'

He frowned. 'If you have a friend among the selkies, I cannot force them to return.'

'No.' Maggie shook her head. 'No. Not a friend. A... my husband. He was swept out to sea yesterday, his boat was capsized—' Maggie bit her lip as the pain tore at her anew, blinking away fresh tears.

'I cannot take what the Sea has claimed.' The selkie man reached out and put a hand on her shoulder. 'All I can do is offer comfort.'

Maggie crumpled and the selkie man caught her. She allowed him to pull her close, resting her head on his chest as a torrent of sobs tore through her body.

After a time her breathing calmed, and he tilted her face up to look at him. His eyes were a soft swirling grey and when his gaze held hers she found she couldn't remember why she'd been so sad.

'Your husband was a good man?' he asked.

Maggie nodded. 'The best.'

'Then be happy you knew him. That you were the one he called wife.' He kissed away a tear that trickled down her cheek.

'What's your name?' she asked.

'Caelan.'

'Caelan.' She liked how the name sounded on her tongue, and when he kissed her full on the lips a warmth spread through her, all memory of her sorrow fading.

She knew she should push him away, but she couldn't remember why. When he laid her down on the damp sand she welcomed his touch.

He was gentle, but all too soon it was over and he was dressing her again in her warm dry clothes and kissing her once more. He picked up his coat and wrapped it around his shoulders, pressing his forehead to hers one last time. But then he pulled the hood over his head, transformed from man to seal, and disappeared into the sea.

With his absence the loss of Hamish tore at her afresh. She pulled her oilskin coat tight around her shoulders, her gaze caught by the distant glow of lanterns coming along the shore.

The villagers were looking for her, and no matter how she might like to join Hamish, she knew she had to go back. But now her sorrow over Hamish was joined by an anguish at the loss of her selkie lover. He'd taken away her sorrow, completely lifted the weight from her shoulders. Could he do it again?

She shook her head. He was a seal, most of the time, and if the stories were right, the seal folk never remembered their human lives. He would have forgotten her already.

Chapter 2

M aggie woke to the empty space in the bed beside her. Hamish's smell lingered in the bed clothes, and she snuggled down into the indent his body had made, imagining for a moment he had simply risen early.

Her heart knew better.

Tears slid down her nose to drip onto the bed.

She'd willingly cry a flood of tears if they would wash her away to Hamish.

She dreaded getting up to face the town. She feared the looks and the whispers, now Hamish was not there to protect her.

A knock sounded on the door, barely a moment before the creak as it opened. Maggie pulled the blanket over her head, wishing whoever it was would go away.

Whoever it was did not go away. Boots swished through the thresh spread across the floor, and a hand came to rest on Maggie's shoulder.

'Tis time to be up, Maggie dear.'

Maggie shook her head.

'Time is passin', lass. And ye need to come and help prepare.'

'I've nothin' to prepare for, Mrs Callanach. No body to wash, to wake, to hold. He's gone.'

'Call me Eilidh, please,' Mrs Callanach said. 'And ye are not the only one to have lost. Those who have bodies to clean have children who need care. It'll do ye no good hiding away here. And why should you have time to grieve when all others have chores to fulfil?

The time for greetin' is comin', but it isna' this morning.'

Maggie winced as Eilidh pulled the blanket back. 'Ye've lost your love. And I know ye fear what's to come, but ye canna let that get in the way of your responsibilities. And your responsibilities are here and now.'

Reluctantly Maggie sat up and allowed Eilidh to pull her from the bed. She ate the cold oats Eilidh spooned into a bowl and followed her out the door.

Outside, the biting wind was already battering the grasses flat, and Maggie pulled her plaid closer around her shoulders.

The walk down the hill passed quickly enough, the muted bustle of the townsfolk soon reaching their ears. But muted as it was, the silence as she stepped onto the cobblestone was deafening.

Eilidh ignored all this, directing Maggie with a firm hand at her elbow, as Maggie dropped her chin to watch the ground pass under her feet.

'Abigail needs her two youngest tending.' Eilidh pulled Maggie to the door of a small bothy, where a woman held a squealing infant, as a toddler wrapped himself around her leg, equally distressed. Her man was stretched out on the table. Abigail looked up as they entered.

'I'm sorry for your loss,' Maggie said, catching Abigail's eye.

'And yours.' Abigail offered a weak smile. 'They havena' found him?'

Maggie shook her head. They'd stopped searching, Abigail must've known that, but then perhaps she was too caught up in her own grief to remember.

Maggie reached out and took the infant from her mother, holding the child upright against her chest and patting her back, singing an old lullaby Maggie's mother had once sung.

The toddler took interest, and Maggie lowered herself into the chair by the fire, allowing the toddler to climb on her knee and nestle into her spare arm.

Maggie watched as Abigail prepared for burial the body of the man she'd loved only a few short years. Eilidh aided Abigail in washing the body and tending the cuts and bruises that would never pain the man now.

There were no tears. Abigail was tender in the way she touched him, and Maggie wondered how she managed it, how she could see her beloved, lifeless in front of her, and stay so strong.

For the rest of the day Maggie followed Eilidh's instructions; caring for children, preparing food, cleaning; the tasks required for day-to day-living were endless. With so many men gone, the few men remaining were digging graves for their brothers and sons. They couldn't help with the women's work. They had grieving of their own to do.

Chapter 3

The lament of the widows echoed around the hills, an eerie backdrop to Maggie's journey to the kirk. She was late, deliberately—she'd wanted to avoid the mingling and small-talk—but now her cheeks burned as she realised every eye would be on her.

She slipped between the heavy oak doors, weaving her way through the bystanders to see the row of men laid out before the altar. Abigail kneeled at the front, her children clinging to their grandmother's skirt. Beside

Abigail were eleven other women, the wives of the others lost. At the end of the row was an empty shroud, for Hamish.

Maggie felt a gentle push from behind and turned to see Eilidh standing there.

'Off ye go, lass. Grieve your man, so he can move on to the next realm.'

Maggie stumbled forward, kneeling beside the keening-woman. She closed her eyes, picturing Hamish's smile, the laughter in his blue eyes. Beside her the keening-woman started again, a cry emerging from some-where deep in her chest, a visceral sound that pulled at the emotion in Maggie, tugging it out of the place she'd squashed it into when she saw how strong Abigail was.

Maggie didn't want to let go, reliving the shame she'd felt when she realised everyone else could hold their emotions better than she. But the keening-woman's skill didn't al-low for any holding, and soon tears drenched Maggie's cheeks and chin as the loss of her dear Hamish bubbled up from inside. As the wails of the other women rose around her,

MAGGIE AND THE SELKIE

Maggie began to rock back and forwards, her tears turning into howls as she pulled at her hair and scratched at her face. Hamish was gone, not even his body remained, and now there was nothing and no one to say goodbye to.

Chapter 4

A fortnight passed. Maggie followed routine; milking the cow, churning the butter, and gathering the eggs. Peat had to be cut for the coming winter, and jumpers needed to be knitted. At night, she snuggled into Hamish's place in the bed and cried herself to sleep. Every morning she woke from dreams of Hamish's miraculous return and found absence.

One morning, Maggie's stomach churned. She brought up her breakfast, and she couldn't stomach supper. As she gathered dulce from the shore, she came upon a dead gull, the waft of its stench sending her heaving long before she came across the decaying corpse. She held her breath as she strode past, heading for the next clump of seaweed to gather into her bag.

When her bleeding time was late, Maggie dismissed it as grief. But as the weeks passed, and the sickness lingered, and her bleeding still didn't come, she couldn't deny the truth.

She hid by collecting the dulce, wandering from the main group to walk alone.

Anything to escape the pitying looks from the village-folk. A new babe, with no father. What terrible timing.

She travelled the beach where she'd walked after that fateful day. It felt somehow weeks ago and also only yesterday, but it wasn't until she came to the burned out remains of a campfire that she thought of the selkie man, Caelan.

Maggie knew of the selkie people, the seal-kin. Stories abounded from olden times, and it was generally accepted that the selkie people still existed, though they had long since abandoned these shores for some other place and time. Too many killed, these days. Too many people greedy for the money the seal skins could bring, and for their oil. It was said there was a great land to the south, where seals outnumbered people, and such products could be gained with ease. Maggie remembered her mother, crossing herself at the talk.

'Those seals are the ones who've escaped from the slaughter on our shores,' Maggie's mother had said. 'Slaughtering them there will bring no good. They've tried to escape us, and if they cannot hide, they'll fight, and those seal bulls are strong on the land, for creatures of the sea.'

Maggie shuddered. Those sea bulls might be strong, and she certainly felt the strength of the man who'd saved her from herself, though he'd been nothing but gentle. She wondered if she could call him again. What had he said? Seven tears into the sea. But

MAGGIE AND THE SELKIE

Maggie found no matter how she tried; she could not summon even one tear to offer the ocean.

Chapter 5

Maggie paced the small cabin, her breath coming in gasps as the squeezing began afresh. She thought she knew what a birthing would bring, thought pains would be eased through breathing and pacing. How wrong she was. Eilidh and Abigail were present, and someone had been sent to summon the midwife, though no one seemed to know where she might be or how long she might take.

Already Maggie had seen the sun set through grasping pain, the full moon travelling to its highest point in a star-filled sky.

The groaning cake had been baked, and Abigail had unknotted every piece of rope and twine and ribbon she could find; sympathetic magic to help ease the baby's passage, but inside her, Maggie's baby seemed to twist and kick, uncertain perhaps, that they even wanted to enter the world.

By the time the midwife arrived, Maggie was on her hands and knees, her bare backside facing the fire as the women watched the dark mess of hair emerge from between her legs.

Eilidh caught the child as it slithered out, slick and greasy, wrapping it in a soft woollen shawl before passing it to Maggie, now sitting up and facing the fire, a blanket around her shoulders.

'A beautiful boy,' Eilidh said, and Maggie's heart melted as she took in the tiny nub of a nose, and the perfect rosebud mouth.

'He's not Hamish's boy,' Abigail muttered. "Not with that mop of dark hair."

'That child is selkie born.' The midwife crossed herself. 'You'll not be cursing a child such as he, lest the ill will of all the seal folk be directed at you.'

Maggie had not wanted to admit such a thing, and yet now the midwife had spoken she knew it to be true. Her child was not Hamish's son, but Caelan's.

'Ronan. That's his name.' The words came to her in a rush, and as soon as they were whispered she wanted to take them back.

Ronan, Little Seal, *my little seal*. Maggie wasn't sure whether to feel repulsed that she'd carried and born the son of a selkie, and not her dear Hamish. But she couldn't deny her feelings for the child. He'd had her heart from the moment she'd felt that first movement inside, and that sense had only grown through the months of movement and response. Learning the child was not Hamish's was upsetting, but it could never strain her affection for the baby.

But Maggie's love for her son was not enough to balance the sorrow of her loss, as sleepless nights compounded the misery of days without Hamish and kept her in swirling darkness not even her child's smiles could break through.

'You need to come out more,' Eilidh urged her. 'Come and visit Abigail; the little ones would love to see the baby; they just dote on him.'

Maggie refused to go. She allowed Eilidh to take Ronan, but she could not leave the house herself. She woke from dreams of waves pulling her under, a little seal swimming by her side.

Perhaps Ronan can become a seal. His father was one, after all. And maybe they would change Maggie into a seal, too, and she and Ronan and Caelan could be a family. And if they could not change her, or would not? She'd be reunited with Hamish, and all would be well again.

Once the thought had entered her mind, Maggie couldn't shake it. Ronan could go back with his family, and she could escape the pitying looks from her neighbours, one way or another.

Chapter 6

For days Maggie walked the shore holding Ronan close as she looked for the best place to put her plan into action.

The obvious place to enter the water was where Caelen had lit his fire, but more than twelve months had passed since that night and any signs of their campfire were long since swept away.

Maggie paced the beach, trying to gauge the location from other landmarks–even stopping to look back to the houses to see if the distance looked right.

She couldn't remember. *Does it matter? The seals travel all the sea.*

'Are you all right, Maggie?'

Maggie twirled around. How had she not seen Abigail walking the length of the beach?

'Are you well?' Abigail put a hand on Maggie's arm.

'I am.' Maggie forced a smile. 'All's well.'

'But you were staring off out to sea, for such a long time. I almost thought...well now, it's foolish. I won't say it out loud. But come back with me now, will you?'

Maggie allowed Abigail to lead her back. Soon, she promised herself, looking out to the sea. Soon.

Chapter 7

Icy water swirled about Maggie's body, pulling on her skirts. She'd expected cold, but not this instant-freezing as she staggered through knee-deep ocean.

Was it too soon to go under? Could she just let the waves pull her down, or should she wade out to where it was deeper?

She called Caelan's name again, but she could hardly hear her own voice over the roar of the sea. How was Caelen ever going to hear her under it?

Ronan squirmed in her arms–a little cocoon of warmth. Maggie stumbled, one hand flung out to steady herself, and the blanket fell away from his head. A sharp sea breeze rustled the small fluffy patch of hair on his head and he let out a squall.

'Hush now.' Maggie pulled the blanket over him, hugging him close. 'It'll be all right, dear one. Shh...you'll be home with your da soon.'

But now Ronan had started his cries wouldn't stop.

'Shush now!' Maggie heard the spit of her tone and tried to hold it back. 'We'll be free from these worries soon enough.'

She took a step, and another, waist deep now. A wave carried the water higher, lifting up over the arm that held Ronan, soaking through her sleeve and his blanket.

He squealed louder.

'Stop! Just stop!'

A hand landed firmly on Maggie's shoulder, and she whirled around, kept upright only by a man's strong grip. It was Davack, Hamish's closest friend.

'Maggie.' Abigail stood on the beach behind Davack, her hands clenched. 'What are ye doin'?'

Maggie shook her head.

Davack reached out for Ronan. 'Give me the lad, Maggie. He'll catch his death.'

'I'm taking him home.' The words were shrieked before she even realised she'd spoken them, and Davack's eyes widened.

He reached out again, and this time his hands closed around the baby.

She pulled away, but his grip was firm, and as Ronan was pulled from her grasp she fell backwards, her final glimpse of Ronan held tight in Davack's strong arms.

Water enveloped her. It seeped through the last layers of clothing, the weight of it sucking her under.

She closed her eyes, accepting whatever might happen next.

Once again Davack's warm hand was on her shoulder, pulling her to the surface, and she kicked and fought and pushed him away, pushing out towards deeper water.

She felt the swell of the ocean now, felt the rise and fall of it, and as the water rose around her once more she kicked, deeper and deeper.

Her chest burned, desperate for air, but she fought against it, fearful of returning to that place, desperate to lose the memories weighing her down.

Something slid past her, warm in the cold. Whiskers brushed her cheek and she opened her eyes as she felt herself once again propelled to the surface.

No! She shook her head, fighting against the creature.

The seal paused, watching her.

You do not want to live? The words were clear in her mind.

She shook her head again. *I want to be free.*

It is a magic that only works once. This is not a choice you can come back from.

Maggie closed her eyes. *Please.*

Caelan nodded, and swam around her, over her, and pushed her again, this time from above.

30

Her lungs bursting for air, there was nothing she could do except open her mouth, but as the bubbles escaped past her face another mouth pressed down on her and hot fishy breath filled her lungs.

Maggie swallowed back the bile that rose in her throat, and as she did a tingle travelled her spine. She floundered in the water as pain fractured her arms and legs, and now Caelan was underneath her, propelling her to the surface, and she couldn't fight him as the pain stole all her senses and then she broke through the surface and now it was the air that pricked her with a million icy fingers and she gasped with the shock of it.

Under water again. It felt warm now, but it wasn't just her sense of the water that had changed, everything had changed.

Her arms and legs were shorter, her body more compact, filled out into a voluptuous, full-fat figure. Her face was contorted, she'd *felt* the whiskers sprout either side of her extended nose – the prickling of pins forcing their way through her skin.

For a moment Maggie was lost; unused to this buoyant figure in the water, free to twist and turn and somersault as she'd never experienced before. She'd *never* felt so graceful.

But then Caelan skimmed past her, and she turned and followed him beyond the breakers, and along the coast until the sea was full of slick, fat creatures, just like herself.

That night Maggie dreamed of a human man and a human child and her heart constricted.

When she woke, all was dark. She blinked, and when her eyes adjusted all she could see were smooth rounded shapes. The briny scent of the sea was strong in her nostrils, the warm bodies compressed tight all around her, protecting her from the cold.

Maggie blinked as the dream faded, wondering about the human figures she'd seemed to care so much about.

As the weight lifted from her shoulders Maggie rested her head back on the sand, and slept.

Thank you for reading!

Thank you for reading!

I hope you enjoyed 'Maggie and the Selkie' the short story prequel to 'What the Tide Brings'.

If you did, and you'd like to keep reading, 'What the Tide Brings' is now available at your favourite online bookstore (or possibly at your local bookshop – quoting the ISBN #: 9780648812418, should help them find it).

Visit https://books2read.com/WhattheTideBrings to find either ebook or print versions!

About the Author

Heather Ewings is an Australian author of speculative fiction. With a Masters in History and a fascination with myth and folklore, Heather's stories explore the past and the present (and occasionally the future) through the lens of the magical. Her short stories have been published in a wide range of places, including Deadset Press, Microcosm, and The Narrative Arc . Heather is a bookworm, a chocoholic, and a would-be hermit (would-be if she didn't need to ferry her children to

their myriad social events). More informa-
tion about Heather and her stories can be
found at www.heatherewings.com.au.

www.ingramcontent.com/pod-product-compliance
Lightning Source LLC
Chambersburg PA
CBHW020535120726
47904CB00003B/1094